SQUISH!

A Wetland Walk

by Nancy Luenn   Illustrated by Ronald Himler

ATHENEUM   1994   NEW YORK

Maxwell Macmillan Canada   *Toronto*

Maxwell Macmillan International   *New York   Oxford   Singapore   Sydney*

Some Books by Nancy Luenn

Nessa's Fish
Mother Earth
Song for the Ancient Forest
Nessa's Story

Illustrated by Ronald Himler

Coyote Dreams
(*by Susan Nunes*)

Atheneum
Macmillan Publishing Company
866 Third Avenue
New York, NY 10022

Maxwell Macmillan Canada, Inc.
1200 Eglinton Avenue East
Suite 200
Don Mills, Ontario M3C 3N1

Macmillan Publishing Company is part of
the Maxwell Communication Group of Companies.

First edition
Printed in Singapore

10 9 8 7 6 5 4 3 2 1

The text of this book is set in Perpetua.
The illustrations are rendered in watercolor.

Library of Congress Cataloging-in-Publication Data

Luenn, Nancy.
   Squish!: a wetland walk / by Nancy Luenn; illustrated by Ronald
Himler. — 1st ed.
      p.   cm.
   ISBN 0–689–31842–1
   1. Wetland ecology—Juvenile literature. 2. Wetlands—Juvenile
literature. [1. Wetlands.   2. Wetland ecology.   3. Ecology.]
I. Himler, Ronald, ill. II. Title.
QH541.5.M3L84   1994
574.5'26325—dc20   93–22628

Splish!
A wetland is a water meadow
It is squishy under boots

It is a place to look for
newts!

and dragonflies

garter snakes

and water striders

A wetland is a place to listen
to a choir of frogs

a blackbird's spring song
the *slap*—of a beaver's tail

It smells like mud
　　and rotting plants
　　and young leaves in a sudden rain

It catches rain and holds it
The water seeps below the ground
    to fill our wells
And we have water through the whole
    dry summer

When autumn comes
  a wetland is a nursery for young salmon
Hidden safe among the reeds
  fingerlings grow ready for their journey to the sea

A wetland can be small

Or as big as the floodplain of a river

When rivers flood
    a wetland slows the water down
    so farms and roads and houses are not washed
    with muddy water

The roots and leaves of wetland plants
help clean the dirty water
They settle silt and filter out pollution

A wetland is a place for hide-and-seek
Mice search for seeds

and heron hunt frogs

Minnows flee from shadows

The precious eggs of dabbling ducks
lie hidden in the weeds

For cattails and willows
   marsh grass and reeds
   salmon and minnows
   dragonflies and water striders

newts and frogs and garter snakes
jumping mice and beavers
blackbirds, heron, ducks, and grebes
A wetland is home

But for us
    it's a marvelous
    muddy
    adventure
Squish!